FLAVORS OF THE WORLD

THE FOOD OF CHINA

Tamra B. Orr

Marshall Cavendish
Benchmark

New York

Website: www.marshallcavendish.us

This publication represents the opinions and views of the author based on Tamra B. Orr's personal experience, knowledge, and research. The information in this book serves as a general guide only. The author and publisher have used their best efforts in preparing this book and disclaim liability rising directly and indirectly from the use and application of this book.

Other Marshall Cavendish Offices:

Marshall Cavendish International (Asia) Private Limited, 1 New Industrial Road, Singapore 536196 • Marshall Cavendish International (Thailand) Co Ltd. 253 Asoke, 12th Flr, Sukhumvit 21 Road, Klongtoey Nua, Wattana, Bangkok 10110, Thailand • Marshall Cavendish (Malaysia) Sdn Bhd, Times Subang, Lot 46, Subang Hi-Tech Industrial Park, Batu Tiga, 40000 Shah Alam, Selangor Darul Ehsan, Malaysia

Marshall Cavendish is a trademark of Times Publishing Limited

All websites were available and accurate when this book was sent to press.

Library of Congress Cataloging-in-Publication Data

Orr, Tamra.
  The food of China / Tamra B. Orr.
        p. cm. — (Flavors of the world)
Includes bibliographical references and index.
Summary: "Explore the culture, traditions, and festivals of China through its food"—Provided by publisher.
ISBN 978-1-60870-234-3 (print)   ISBN 978-1-60870-687-7 (ebook)

1. Food habits—China—Juvenile literature. 2. Festivals—China—Juvenile literature. 3. China—Social life and customs—Juvenile literature. I. Title.

GT2853.C6077 2012
394.1'20951—dc22
2010039293

Editor: Christine Florie
Publisher: Michelle Bisson
Art Director: Anahid Hamparian
Series Designer: Kay Petronio

Expert Reader: Ina Asim, Historian of China, University of Oregon, Eugene

Photo research by Marybeth Kavanagh
Cover photo by Yadid Levy/Alamy
The photographs in this book are used by permission and through the courtesy of: *Alamy*: Bon Appetit, 4; TAO Images Limited, 9, 26, 44; Dennis Cox, 20, 28; Lou Linwei, 29; Jon Arnold Images Ltd, 31; Danita Delimont, 35; Michele Burgess, 37; Neil Setchfield/yuckfood.com, 40; Argus Photo, 49; Japanese Foods, 50; Eitan Simanor, 55; *The Image Works*: Panorama Images, 8, 41, 51; Ellen B. Senisi, 19; Lee Snider, 30; Alain Evrard/Impact/HIP, 38; Ji Yukun/Panorama, 46; Bill Lai, 57; *Getty Images*: Mahaux Photography, 11; China Photos, 21; Kim Steele/Image Bank, 32; *SuperStock*: Flirt, 12; Prisma, 23, 56; *The Bridgeman Art Library*: FuZhai Archive, 16; *Fotolia*: Akhilesh Sharma (banner), front cover, 1, 3, 5, 18, 27, 43, 53; Sandra Cunningham (spices), 10, 24, 34, 45, 54; Tomboy2290 (bok choy), 3; Norman Chan (egg roll), front & back cover, 1, 64; *Shutterstock*: Suto Norbert Zsolt (map), front cover, 1, 2-3, 9, 14, 20, 23, 25, 37, 40, 42, 47, 48, 55, 57; *VectorStock*: Nicemonkey (plate), back cover, 3

Maps (pp. 6 and 22) by Mapping Specialists Limited

Printed in Malaysia (T)

1 3 5 6 4 2

CONTENTS

ONE

Welcome to China!

If you are planning for a year, sow rice; if you are planning for a decade, plant trees; if you are planning for a lifetime, educate people.

—Chinese proverb

A quick glance at the globe is all that's needed to find China. As the fourth-largest country in the world (after Russia, Canada, and the United States), it covers 3.7 million square miles (9.6 million square kilometers). It is the most populous country in the world, with 1.3 billion people—four times more than the United States. That many people require a great deal of food— and China's history is rich with tales of how it has managed to grow enough to feed all of those mouths. People with abundant water supplies found ways to use land for rice paddies and

The Chinese developed a cuisine rich in variety, flavor, and appearance.

TOPOGRAPHICAL MAP OF CHINA

RUSSIA

KAZAKHSTAN

MONGOLIA

KYRGYZSTAN

GOBI DESERT

TAJIKISTAN

AFGHANISTAN

PAKISTAN

Beijing

NORTH KOREA

CHINA

Yellow Sea

Huai River

Yangzi River

Yangzi Valley

East China Sea

BHUTAN

NEPAL

Mt. Everest

INDIA

INDIA

PACIFIC OCEAN

TAIWAN

MYANMAR

VIETNAM

LAOS

Zhujiang Delta

THAILAND

South China Sea

6 The Food of China

open fields for wheat. They developed cooking techniques and preparation methods that made the food stretch further and last longer. Finally, they turned the art of cooking into the art of creating **cuisine** and, in doing so, produced dishes that looked and smelled as wonderful as they tasted.

Landforms

China has thousands of miles of coastline, bordering the Pacific Ocean, the Yellow Sea, the East China Sea, and the South China Sea. More than five thousand islands are scattered across these waters, the largest of which is Taiwan. The land has many rivers, including the Yangzi, the third-longest river in the world. Because of its size, China shares borders with more than a dozen countries: Mongolia, Russia, North Korea, Vietnam, Laos, Myanmar, Bhutan, Nepal, India, Pakistan, Afghanistan, Tajikistan, Kyrgyzstan, and Kazakhstan.

Covering such a vast area, China has almost every possible type of landform. It has forest steppes and subtropical forests. It has snowy mountaintops such as Mount Everest and arid regions such as the Gobi Desert. More than 60 percent of the land is made up of hills, mountains, and plateaus. Long, snaking rivers cross the land, and seaports line the coastlines. In the south, water is used by people to get from one region to another as well as to irrigate fields.

The lush northern region of China is covered with grain fields. Over the centuries, these fields have been used to grow wheat. The flour made from the wheat was used to make noodles that the region was—and still is—famous for. The southern and eastern

China's northern region supports hearty fields of wheat.

A Deep-Fried Ghost for Breakfast

One of the most popular breakfast street foods throughout China is *youtiao* or *yau ja gwai*, meaning "deep-fried ghosts." These slightly sweet treats are similar to scones or crullers and were named in honor of Yue Fei, a national hero who was imprisoned by Qin Hui, an official people thought of as an "evil ghost."

regions are close to oceans full of endless types of seafood, which are included in many traditional Chinese dishes.

Although China is huge, only a small portion, about 15 percent, is suitable for growing food. The rest of it is too dry, too wet, or too rocky. This lack of fertile land, coupled with the nation's

Fried Rice

There are few dishes that better represent the Chinese diet than fried rice. It's a great way to use the rice, meat, and vegetables left over from a previous meal. Fried rice is simple and can serve as a snack or main dish—or, if there is only a little left, it can be thrown into a stir-fry. Be sure to get an adult's help with the chopping and cooking!

Makes 4–5 servings

Ingredients

4 cups cooked long-grain white rice, cold
2 tablespoons vegetable oil
½ cup onion, chopped
2 eggs, beaten
2 tablespoons soy sauce

Directions

Use a fork to fluff and separate the grains of cooked rice. With an adult's help, put a large skillet or a wok over high heat. Add 1 tablespoon of the oil. Add the chopped onion and cook until it is a light golden brown. Remove from the wok and set aside. Heat the remaining 1 tablespoon of oil in the skillet or wok and add the eggs. Stir until cooked. Add the rice and stir in the soy sauce. Add the onion back in, and mix thoroughly with the other ingredients until everything is hot. Remove from the heat and serve.

massive population, has created a history of food shortages. Those shortages, in turn, have affected how the Chinese prepare and eat their food.

The small percentage of land that does support agriculture is used to its fullest. For thousands of years, tea plants have been grown and harvested. Tea grows best in rainy regions with an

Tea plants are an ancient crop grown in certain regions of China. Tea is a part of most meals.

altitude of 2,100 to 7,000 feet (600 to 2,100 meters), so it does quite well in parts of China. More than two hundred types of tea are produced, including green, yellow, white, black, and oolong. Tea is the main beverage consumed in China, and most people there drink many cups a day. The country also exports $100 million worth of tea every year to other countries.

Some Chinese farmers grow rice in terraced fields.

Another common use of land in the more fertile regions of China is for growing rice. Most rice paddies are found in the Yangzi valley, south of the Huai River, and in the Zhujiang delta. Rice paddies require huge amounts of water. Therefore, rice must be grown near rivers and lakes, or dependable irrigation systems must be in place. Rice is the foundation of the Chinese diet, and many families keep 100-pound (45-kilogram) bags in their kitchens at all times.

Climate

Since China covers such a large area, it also has a wide variety of climates. Temperatures range from extreme highs of over 100 degrees Fahrenheit (38 degrees Celsius) in the desert regions to bitterly cold winter lows of –13 °F (–25 °C) in the northeastern regions. One of the most important influences on the weather are the **monsoons**, winds that blow during certain seasons. During the winter, cold, dry air gusts across Central Asia and across China to the sea. From late spring through early autumn, the winds blow in the opposite direction, bringing warm, humid air from the sea to inland areas. It is these months that bring the most rain to China.

Although the desert areas commonly see less than 4 inches (10 centimeters) of rain per year, other areas in China receive far more. In the north, 25 to 40 inches (64 to 102 cm) may fall annually; in the south, it is more likely to be double that, with up to 80 inches (203 cm) falling per year.

The temperature extremes, combined with the lack of rain in many areas and the rocky terrain, make growing large amounts of crops very challenging. Despite progress in irrigation technology and endless hard work, it is still difficult for farmers to continuously grow bountiful crops.

Culture and History

China is home to one of the oldest civilizations in the world. Experts believe that people have lived in the region for almost

Yin and Yang

One of China's oldest beliefs is in the balance between the forces of yin and yang. First mentioned around 500 BCE in the book *I Ching* (or *Book of Changes*), written by the philosopher Confucius, the idea revolves around creating balance in everything from relationships to architecture. Keeping this ideal in mind, Chinese cooks strive for balance when preparing food. They want harmony between the food's color, flavor, and texture. This is the main reason for cooking sweet and sour dishes—and for combining foods such as cabbage and beef or carrots and chicken.

2 million years. A prehistoric group called the Beijing people lived there 600,000 years ago, and by about 8,000 BCE, the area was populated by several different cultures.

From the very beginning of Chinese civilization, the people relied on farming. Millet and rice were cultivated, chickens and pigs were domesticated, and some of the land was used to raise cattle and sheep. For thousands of years, the people were ruled by **aristocratic** families known as **dynasties**. These families gave specific names to their time of rule. The first imperial dynasty was the Qin (221–206 BCE), from which China most likely got its name.

Over time, the dynasties changed as battles for control were waged between ruling families. During the Ming dynasty (1368–1644 CE), millions of fruit trees were planted, and crops of sweet potatoes, corn, and sugarcane were introduced. Ever since **Buddhism** spread throughout China, followers of the religion have preferred a vegetarian diet. They grew soybeans and used them to make **tofu**, or bean curd, since it provides great amounts of protein, similar to meat. Wheat and rice were ground into flour and made into noodles.

The age of imperial dynasties in China ended in 1911, when the country became a **republic**. In 1949 the People's Republic of China was proclaimed. Today, China is one of the busiest nations in the world. Despite its lack of fertile land, about 40 percent of all China's workers are farmers. Besides rice, the country produces more apples, cotton, pears, potatoes, tobacco, and wheat than any

This thirteenth-century painting depicts the planting of rice.

other country. It grows almost all of the world's supply of sweet potatoes. In the south, farmers grow more exotic crops, including bananas, oranges, and pineapples. Most farms also have quite a few ducks and hogs, and some even have cattle, goats, horses, and sheep. Thanks to the ocean, as well as the many rivers and

lakes throughout China, farmers and fishers are able to catch millions of tons of fish and shellfish every year.

China's history is long and full of memorable events and people. Its heritage is found in the amazing variety of food that has been part of the Chinese people's lives and culture for centuries.

TWO

The Regions of China

To the ruler, people are heaven; to the people, food is heaven.

—Chinese proverb

Although the Chinese people share many foods—especially tea, rice, and noodles—there is great variety from one region to the next. The differing temperatures and weather patterns across the vast country affect what can and cannot be grown. Because of this, the types of food being prepared and eaten changes tremendously as you travel from one end of the country to the other.

From Region to Region

Some professional chefs might argue that there are more than a dozen different styles of cooking found throughout China. Most agree that there are five primary cuisine regions.

The first region is located in the northern area, where people must deal with extreme temperature changes. Their winters are very cold, while their summers are hot and dry. Rice cannot

Homemade dough is filled to make dumplings, a favorite treat in China.

grow well there, so wheat is cultivated instead. The people use wheat flour to make many different dishes, including noodles, steamed dumplings, and pancakes. Recipes often include leeks, onions, and garlic to keep the body warm in the cold winter. This style of cooking is often referred to as Beijing cuisine, because the capital of the region, Beijing, is located at its center. In this region, the famous Beijing duck was invented. It was originally made to please the emperor. Another popular dish in this area is Mongolian hot pot, which usually contains mutton (lamb).

Hand-Pulled Noodles

When taking a walk along most busy city streets in Lanzhou (in north-western China), you will almost certainly be offered a taste of the local favorite, Lanzhou beef noodles. Watch as cooks pull and stretch these noodles, wrapping them up until they look like a coil of rope. Then they toss them into hot water for a minute or two. Add beef broth and pour into a bowl, and you have a hot, tasty snack to go.

The second region with its own cuisine is in eastern China, where the vast majority of the nation's population lives. There you will find meals made with both wheat and rice, and noodles are always a favorite. Because this area has so many rivers, including the Yangzi, and a long coastline, fish and seafood are often included in meals. In southeastern China, Fujian cuisine features these items. The Shanghai hairy crab is a favorite treat. Wild mushrooms grow here and are frequently added to recipes. Egg rolls, an Asian treat found all over the world today, got their start there.

If you have a sweet tooth, this is the area to be in, as there are a number of sugarcane plantations. More sugar is used in the east than in any other part of China. Pastries are popular here.

The southern region of China is home to Cantonese cooking. Chances are, if you go to a Chinese restaurant in the United States, this is the style of cooking you will find. Stir-frying is the favorite method used in Cantonese cooking. Most dishes feature the day's catch, such as shrimp, lobster, and eels. Fertile farms provide fresh vegetables. Sweet and sour dishes, as well as fried rice recipes, began in this region. Sauces often include both soy and ginger, and dishes include barbecued meat and **dim sum**.

Many Chinese enjoy steamed hairy crabs when they are in season.

THE FOOD REGIONS OF CHINA

CHINA

Chili peppers		Oxen		Sugarcane	
Crab		Wild mushrooms		Tea	
Eels		Rice		Vegetable crops	
Fish		Shrimp		Wheat	
Lobster					

Marvelous Mushrooms

For thousands of years, the Chinese have used mushrooms in their dishes. In the late twentieth century, China grew hundreds of thousands of tons of mushrooms and was the world's leading producer. More than half

the world's varieties of mushrooms and fungi are found in this country, including the shiitake, the straw mushroom, and the tree ear, a flat, ear-shaped mushroom that grows from the trunk of a tree and is firm but crunchy.

The western region of China has produced a style of cooking called Sichuan. Grab some tea and a fan when you eat dishes from this region. The west is often hot and humid, so the people deal with it by eating spicy food that makes them sweat. Sweat evaporates and cools a person down. In the sixteenth century, the spiciness of the area's food increased with the addition of chili peppers. These were introduced by Portuguese traders, who brought them to China from South Asia. Today, many peppers and Sichuan peppercorns—berries from a prickly ash tree—are

Chinese Cabbage

Many of the people in China are Buddhists and, in following that belief, they are vegetarians who do not eat any meat. Vegetarian recipes are common in Chinese cooking and vary from vegetable stir-fries to meals made using tofu as a substitute for meat. Here is a simple recipe based on one of the most typical vegetables. You will need an adult to help you slice the cabbage.

Serves 4

Ingredients

1 pound Chinese cabbage
½ cup canned vegetable broth
1 tablespoon cornstarch
2 tablespoons vegetable oil
1 teaspoon salt

Directions

Wash the cabbage and dry it with paper towels. Cut it in half, discarding the core. Slice the rest of the cabbage into 1-inch pieces. Mix the broth and cornstarch together. Set aside.

With an adult's help, heat the oil in a skillet or wok. Add the cabbage and salt and stir-fry for about 4 minutes. Add the cornstarch mixture, stir everything well, and cook for about 30 seconds. Remove from the heat and serve.

grown in the western part of China. Recipes often include garlic, leek, and onion. Hot and sour soup is always on the menu.

The last region, located in central China, is known as the home of Hunan cooking. In many ways, it is similar to Sichuan cuisine because it uses quite a few hot spices and fresh chili peppers. Because of Hunan's central location, however, its people have access to many other types of food as well. The province is sometimes called the land of rice and fishes. The region's fertile, rolling hills support many different crops. Dongting Lake, the second-largest lake in China, is home to a variety of fish and turtles, which are also included in Hunan recipes.

A Modern Chinese Cook

In 2006 a new kind of Chinese cook was introduced at the China High Tech Fair in Shenzhen. Like most Chinese cooks, this one was able to make a delicious dish of kung pao chicken, but it was prepared in less than two minutes. This cook was AIC, which stands for Artificial Intelligent Cooking. It is a robot that is able to steam, stir-fry, and make thousands of traditional Chinese recipes in a matter of minutes. AIC's inventor is Liu Xinyu, and he hopes that some day homes and restaurants throughout China will have one of his robots in the kitchen.

Assorted dried chili pepper flakes and peppercorns are sold in a local Sichuan market.

Perhaps the most unusual aspect of Hunan cuisine is the lengthy preparation that goes into many of its dishes. Many of them require hours of hard work, including orange beef, which has to marinate overnight, and crispy duck, which is made by steaming and then deep frying. Finally, before serving, the dishes are decorated so that they look as good as they taste.

THREE

Have You Eaten Yet?

If one hopes to become a good cook, he must first become a good matchmaker; the flavors and ingredients must be "married" and "harmonized."

—Chinese proverb

One look at the Chinese language reveals how important the role food plays in its culture. People often greet each other with the question "*Chi fan le mei you*?" which means "Have you eaten yet?" The word for rice is *fan*, which also means "food." When the Chinese write characters (instead of letters), the ones used for lunch translate to "midday rice," while the characters for dinner mean "evening rice."

Rice, Tea, and Noodles

No matter what kitchen you peek into in China, you are certain to find three things: rice, noodles, and tea. They form the foundation of every meal in every household.

Rice is a staple in the Chinese diet.

The average Chinese person eats four bowls of rice every day. The way it is prepared changes with each recipe and from one region to another, but it is almost always placed in the center of the table. Sometimes the rice is boiled or steamed. Other times it is added to soup. The grain is turned into flour, vinegar, and even wine. Although there are many different types of rice available, the kind most commonly found on a family kitchen table is unseasoned, long-grain white rice.

Every meal, as well as mid–morning and mid–afternoon snacks, is accompanied by a pot of hot tea, although the tea is not drunk with the food, but after it. Thousands of people are employed to pick and prepare the leaves that make the tea used throughout China and imported around the world.

Tea has been important to the Chinese people for thousands of years. In ancient China, the aristocracy hired special tea masters to supervise the preparation of the beverage. Even today, the Chinese are very particular about how their tea is served. First, water is heated to the boiling point and poured into an empty teapot. This heats the pot itself. This water is then thrown out. Next, dried tea leaves are placed inside the pot. Then new water

A tea-shop owner prepares tea following the Chinese tea ceremony ritual.

is heated to the boiling point, and added to **steep** the tea. The Chinese feel it destroys the fine aroma of the tea to add anything to it, such as milk, lemon, or sugar, so they drink it hot and plain.

Another staple food found in many parts of China is noodles, or *mein*. They vary in width and can be as thin as needles or as thick as pencils. They are almost always long, however, because to the Chinese, long noodles are a symbol of long life. Chinese noodles are made from wheat or rice flour, depending on whether you are in northern or southern China. There are more than one thousand varieties of noodles eaten throughout the country. They are prepared in many different ways: boiled, steamed, deep-fried, or added to soup. Some people prefer them hot, others cold.

Of course, a diet that consists of just noodles and rice, with a hot cup of tea on the side, would not be enough to fill a hungry stomach or provide enough nutrients, which is why the Chinese also include a wide variety of vegetables in their diets. Typically, a person in China eats five

Along with rice, noodles, or *mein*, are served throughout China.

Vegetables make up a large portion of Chinese dishes. Fresh produce can be bought at local outdoor markets.

servings of vegetables a day. Many of the vegetables used in China are the same ones used in other parts of the world, but some are quite interesting by U.S. standards. Among the favorites are water chestnuts, lotus and taro roots, bamboo shoots, bok choy, and bean sprouts. Some dishes might include exotic ingredients such as lily buds or blossoms, or a fungus called cloud ear. It is a jellylike fungus that grows on dead wood and is said to have a unique, crunchy feel.

Fried, decorated carp will become the centerpiece at a celebration table.

Other common ingredients found in Chinese kitchens include eggs, fish, and tofu. The eggs may come from chickens, but they also may come from ducks, geese, pigeons, and quail. Fish is an important ingredient in many recipes and is served during festivals; the fish is often the centerpiece of the table. Not only do the Chinese like its flavor, but the fish also symbolizes abundance and wealth. During feasts, whole fish are put on the table, and the head is pointed at the guest of honor as a sign of respect. Tofu is often referred to as "meat without bones." It is an excellent source of nutrition and comes in different textures, so it can be used in everything from main dishes to desserts. Soybeans, used to make tofu, are also used in making marinades, dips, and soy sauce, a popular seasoning added to most dishes.

Time for Soup

The Chinese love soup. It is fairly quick and easy to prepare, and it uses up the last bits of meat, grain, and vegetables left over from other dishes. A long history of food shortages has taught the people of China to stretch what food they have and use everything.

Soup is not just an appetizer or side dish in China, as it is in many parts of the United States. It is considered a main dish and is often prepared with meat, bones, eggs, fish, vegetables, fruits, and mushrooms. Some of the soups have thin broths and limited ingredients, while others are like thick stews, with chunky ingredients. Often, soup is the only beverage served with a meal, and typically it is eaten last, because the Chinese believe it helps with digestion.

A favorite type of soup in China is called hot and sour soup. It is made with chicken broth, peppers, soy sauce, rice vinegar, ginger, bamboo shoots, green onions, and tofu. Soup is commonly used as medicine in China, too, especially to fight simple colds and the flu. Not only is hot soup considered comforting but, in some cases, the ingredients are thought to be healing.

A Peek Inside the Kitchen

Take one look at a typical Chinese kitchen, and you'll realize that the methods of cooking are much different than those of the United States. Instead of appliances such as microwaves

Egg Drop Soup

This traditional soup is one of the most popular dishes throughout China. It is inexpensive to make and uses some of the most common ingredients in the country. It is a warming soup, full of protein and nutrition. Be sure an adult helps in the preparation.

Serves 4

Ingredients

4 cups chicken stock

½ teaspoon grated ginger

1 tablespoon soy sauce

4 green onions, chopped (one set aside for garnish)

¾ cup mushrooms, sliced

¼ teaspoons white pepper

1 tablesspoon corn starch

3 eggs, lightly beaten

Directions

Place ½ cup of the chicken stock aside.

Place the remainder of the chicken stock, ginger, soy sauce, green onions, mushrooms, and pepper in a soup pot over medium heat and bring to a boil. Add the corn starch to the reserved chicken stock and mix well. Add the mixture to the soup pot, stir, and then turn the heat down to a simmer. Slowly pour in the beaten eggs while still stirring the soup. The egg will spread throughout the soup like yellow ribbons. Turn off the heat and garnish with reserved green onions. Serve hot.

and ovens, a Chinese kitchen is much more likely to have a wok, wooden cutting boards, a rice cooker, and bamboo steamers. Instead of forks, knives, spoons, and large dinner plates on the table, people use chopsticks, porcelain spoons, and a number of bowls. While sharp knives are found in the cooking area, none are used at the table.

A wok is one of the most used objects in any Chinese kitchen. Typically made out of aluminum or steel, woks can be used to stir-fry, steam, deep-fry, boil, **simmer**, **braise**, or smoke food. Shaped like a large bowl, woks range in size from 9 to 24 inches (23 to 61 cm) in diameter. A family tends to use one of medium size,

Woks are a common household cooking utensil in many Chinese homes.

between 12 and 14 inches (30 and 36 cm) in diameter. In large restaurants, huge woks are placed over roaring fires. The cook has to pay close attention so that nothing burns during cooking as the wok is tipped and turned and the ingredients stirred. The wok is kept in constant motion.

Many Chinese people, especially those living in the largest cities, go to supermarkets to do their shopping, just as people do in the United States. But those in smaller cities or living on farms get their food through other methods, including growing it, going to local food markets, or buying it from street vendors. Market stalls feature fresh fish, vegetables, fruit, and more, and they are a lively and interesting place to buy food. Farmers often have simple diets based on what they can produce on their land, and they eat little meat. Processed foods are rarely found in the rural areas of China. Instead, meals are usually composed of a grain and vegetables.

A Seat at the Table

If you take a seat at a Chinese table, it is easy to notice that the settings look different. Instead of a large plate, several small bowls are set in front of each diner for rice, meat, and vegetables. The food is eaten with chopsticks, which may be made of wood, bamboo, plastic, bone, or ivory. They are held like a pair of pincers, with the bottom stick staying still and the top one moving back and forth in order to pick up bits of food. A special flat-bottomed porcelain spoon is provided for eating soup.

A Land of Invention

The Chinese are known for some of the world's best inventions, including ice cream. Three thousand years ago, it was made out of milk and rice and packed in snow. Some royal chefs mixed snow and ice and added fruit, wine, and honey to make a special treat for Chinese rulers. The explorer Marco Polo took the recipe to Italy with him, and it spread from there.

Rural Chinese purchase their food at local outdoor markets.

When the food is brought to the table, the rice usually is set in the center in a large bowl. Smaller bowls filled with fish or meat and vegetables are placed around it. Most meals are considered communal. Families gather to share the food directly from these bowls, reaching out with their chopsticks. Because tables are usually round, everybody can reach all dishes, but it is not considered bad manners if someone needs to reach across the table

A family shares a traditional Chinese meal.

to pick up food from a platter. Napkins typically consist of hot towels distributed at the end of the meal. Drinks and desserts are rarely found at the Chinese dinner table.

If a single grain of rice is left in a guest's bowl, it means that the guest did not like the food—and that the guest has forgotten to show respect for the labor that went into preparing it. It is also considered bad manners to eat the last little piece of fish from the serving bowl. A host will think that his or her guest is still hungry because he or she did not prepare enough.

Chop Long, Cook Short

Many Chinese recipes take much longer to prepare than they do to actually cook. This comes from a long history of having very limited fuel sources. A lack of dry wood meant fires burned for a brief time, so food had to be cooked quickly. To make the most of what they had, cooks would spend their time chopping meat and vegetables into bite-size pieces that would cook quickly and evenly when added to the oil in a hot pot such as a wok. This technique became known as stir-frying because the food has to be constantly stirred to keep it from burning. Often only a few minutes go by between the cooking and the serving.

A Sight—and Sound—to Behold

The Chinese believe that food should do more than taste good. They believe it must also smell and look good. They focus on presenting beautiful as well as tasty dishes. In ancient China,

Eggs, Anyone?

Two of China's most interesting egg recipes are salted duck eggs and century eggs (right).

Salted duck eggs are made by soaking the eggs in brine, or salty water, for a month. The yolk soaks up the liquid and turns a bright orange-red. Century eggs are soaked in a mixture of ash, salt, lime, clay, and rice straw for about three months. The egg white turns dark brown, and the yolk becomes creamy and dark green. Not surprisingly, the eggs have a strong taste that has been compared to cheese.

arranging the food on the plates of royalty was an important task for artisans, who carved intricate designs into melons, carrots, and other types of food.

Today, Chinese chefs rarely take that much time, except for those working in fancy restaurants. But every chef makes an effort to combine bright colors and shapes. Chefs also tend to add **garnishes** to food to enhance its appearance. These include sesame seeds, rings of green onion, sprigs of cilantro, slices of cucumber and tomatoes, pieces of fruit or a few delicate mint or basil leaves. The only rules for a garnish are that it look lovely, provide contrast, and be edible!

To make each dish perfect, the chef has to give it a special name. Often the names are inspired by the dish's shape and

To the Chinese, food should look as good as it tastes.

appearance, rather than the main ingredients. Stir-fried chicken with broccoli is called jade flower chicken. Pork meatballs are called lion's heads. Some dishes are named after famous Chinese people, such as Su Dongpo's pork (he is a famous Chinese poet and scholar). Giving a recipe a beautiful or witty name helps make the meal more enjoyable and memorable.

Too Good to Miss

One of the oddest names for a dish in China is Buddha jumps over the wall. Legend has it that the meal got its name because, one day long ago, Buddha was walking past a wall when he smelled something so delicious and wonderful that he could not resist tracking it down. Jumping over the wall, he landed in a family's yard, where the special dish was just being served. He sat down and joined them—and they named the food made out of shark's fin after him.

Feast and Fun

||||||||||||||||||||||||||||||||||||||||||||||||||||||||||||||||||||||||||||||||||

If one eats less, one will taste more.

—Chinese proverb

Since food is so important to the Chinese, it makes sense that holidays and celebrations mean fancy costumes, fun games, and amazing feasts. From the Chinese New Year to the Lantern Festival, from weddings to birthdays, the right kind of food plays a big role.

Birthdays are often celebrated by eating long noodles in soup. The longer the noodle, it is believed, the longer the life of the person eating it. New babies, on the other hand, are welcomed with a seaweed soup called black moss. It looks like strands of black hair and is supposed to be especially healthy for new mothers.

Virtually all Chinese weddings include a huge banquet and feature a whole roasted pig and small, individual Chinese wedding cakes. At many weddings, the dragon and phoenix (which represent male and female) are symbolized through food. For example, the dragon is represented by lobster or eel, and the phoenix by chicken.

The Chinese Lantern Festival, which is held on the fifteenth day of the first lunar month of the year, always features little round dumplings called *tang yuan*. A sweet treat, they are made from rice flour and are boiled in water. Some are dipped in syrup, while others have sweet fillings. During the Dragon Boat Festival, people eat *zongzi*, steamed rice dumplings wrapped in bamboo leaves. Some have meat, nuts, vegetables, dates, or fruit inside and are dipped in sugar or honey.

Women prepare zongzi, steamed rice wrapped in bamboo leaves.

Chinese Dumplings

Called *jiaozi* in China, these dumplings make soup a full meal. They are usually a part of the Chinese New Year celebrations, their fillings change depending on what people like. In China, making dumplings is something families do together. Serve them in your favorite broth. If you make them, be sure to have an adult help you.

Serves 4

Ingredients for dough

2 cups white flour

4 teaspoons baking powder

1 teaspoon salt

4 tablespoons butter, softened

1 cup milk

Ingredients for filling

1 cup ground pork

1 tablespoon soy sauce

¼ teaspoon ground white pepper

3 tablespoon sesame oil

½ onion, minced

1 ½ cups shredded Napa cabbage

1 teaspoon ginger

1 clove garlic, minced

Directions

Combine flour, baking powder, and salt in a mixing bowl. Incorporate butter. Add milk until a moist dough is formed. Cover mixing bowl and let dough rest while you prepare the filling.

To begin the filling, mix soy sauce and white pepper into the ground pork. Add the rest of the ingredients to the pork mixture and combine well.

Divide the dough into fifty small pieces, rolling each into three inch diameter disks. Place 1 tablespoon of filling in the center of one disk, folding the dough completely over the filling. Pinch the edges together to seal. Continue until all the disks of dough are filled.

Prepare your favorite broth according to directions and bring to a strong simmer. Carefully drop dumplings into the broth with a teaspoon. Cover and simmer for 10 minutes or until the dumplings are fully cooked.

Serve and enjoy!

To make a sweeter dumpling, replace the meet filling with raisins, chopped apples, and/or nuts and cinnamon.

Moon cakes are eaten during the Mid-Autumn Festival.

During the Moon or Mid-Autumn Festival, celebrated on the fifteenth day of the eighth lunar month, the Chinese snack on a treat called moon cakes. This pastry varies from one region to another. In the east, it has a crisp, flaky crust and is shaped into a round, white disk that looks like the moon. In the south, on the other hand, a thinner crust is made, and the outside is brushed with egg whites to make it shine. Fillings range from red bean paste, lotus seed paste, and salty duck egg yolks to fruits, nuts, and meats.

Happy New Year!

Without a doubt, the biggest holiday celebration in China is the Chinese New Year, or Spring Festival. It is a fifteen-day festival full of feasting. The family dinner on New Year's Eve is considered the most important meal of the year, and the family often saves up for months in order to make the fanciest dishes they can. Kitchen tables are covered from end to end with some of the most elegant and exotic dishes Chinese cuisine has to offer.

Some of the more commonly prepared dishes are fried meatballs, fish, chicken, New Year's cakes, pomelo, and candied fruits and melons. Each of them has a symbolic meaning. The round fruits and cakes represent the unity of the family, and the other

Seeing Red

Red is a lucky color in China, which is why it can be spotted everywhere during festivals and birthdays. The Chinese flag is almost completely red, and so are the envelopes presented to children on New Year's Eve. Traditional wedding dresses are also bright red. One month after a baby is born in China, some families host a "red egg and ginger party." Hard-boiled eggs are dyed red and handed out to guests.

dishes express what the family hopes for in the coming year. Two of the most difficult dishes to prepare for New Year's are Beijing duck and shark fin soup.

Chinese fried meatballs, or *rou wan*, are made from ground pork. However, instead of being seasoned with garlic, oregano, and basil as Italian-style meatballs are, in China they are flavored with ginger and soy sauce. They symbolize family togetherness. A whole fish, complete with head and tail, is made in the hopes that the family will not lack for anything in the coming year.

A sweet dessert called *nian gao*, or New Year's cake, is a sticky, chewy treat made from rice flour. Some are made from wheat flour and are much fluffier. Both stand for prosperity and success in the new year. Pomelo, a fruit similar to grapefruit only sweeter, is served. Candied fruits and melons are given out to guests to wish them good health, fertility, harmony, prosperity, and success. Foods such as these—as well as pistachios, melon seeds dyed

Bring on the Bubbles

Look in the bottom of the glass holding some Chinese drinks, and you will see brightly colored bubbles. They are actually tiny balls made from tapioca, the root of the cassava plant. They are used in pudding and as a thickener, or sweetened and mixed into drinks to add calcium.

A candy box is full of fruit, sweets, and other treats for the Chinese New Year.

red, peanuts, coconut, and dried fruit—are shared with family and friends. Nothing bitter or sour is allowed, so that nothing unpleasant will happen during the new year.

Complex and Controversial Cuisine

Two of the most complicated dishes prepared during Chinese festivals and celebrations are Beijing duck and shark fin soup.

The recipe for Beijing duck dates back more than six centuries. Cooks from all over China traveled to Beijing to cook for the emperor. Only the very best chefs were allowed into the royal kitchens. One of the dishes developed there was Beijing duck. The recipe was kept secret until the last imperial dynasty ended in 1911. Then court chefs took their skills and special recipes and started their own restaurants.

To make this dish, cooks must first pump air under the skin of the duck to separate it from the meat. Next, the skin is coated with a sweet sauce and hung out to dry in the open air for ten hours.

Beijing duck is a famous dish prized for the thin, crispy skin of roasted duck.

Shark fin soup is an expensive delicacy served in China.

Finally, it is hung in a brick oven and baked until the meat is tender and the skin is crispy. When it is done, the duck is cut into as many as one hundred thin slices. It is served with light steamed pancakes, scallions, and an aromatic sauce.

Shark fin soup has been part of Chinese cuisine for hundreds of years. It is a delicacy that is quite expensive to prepare—dried shark fins can cost hundreds of dollars a pound. It is labor intensive as well. The dried fin has to be soaked in water for hours to soften, then it is added to a pot of ham, garlic, green onions, and chicken broth to cook for three hours to add flavor, because the shark fin itself doesn't have a particular taste. Just before the soup is finished, the ham is taken out, and cornstarch is added to thicken the broth. Finally, it is spooned into bowls, topped with bean sprouts, and served.

Serving this soup is considered a way to show respect for a special guest and to demonstrate wealth in China. However, in recent years, the practice has been condemned by many conservation groups. More than 38 million sharks are killed each year just for their fins, which is bringing them closer and closer to extinction.

FIVE

Staying Healthy

To extend your life by a year, take one less bite each meal.

—Chinese proverb

Centuries of dealing with food shortages have taught many Chinese the importance of eating carefully and with great thought. They have found ways to make their food the healthiest and most nutritious possible.

Because it includes an average of five vegetable servings a day, the Chinese diet is often quite healthy. Cooks do not rely on canned or frozen vegetables, either. They highly value fresh produce instead. Most cooks will go to the market every day in order to get the freshest and best ingredients for their dishes. Some companies even allow their employees half-hour shopping breaks during the course of the workday so they can dash out and get what they need for their family meal.

When cooking produce at home, the Chinese focus on steaming or stir-frying vegetables rather than boiling them. This preserves not only the vegetables' colors but also their vitamins and minerals.

Chicken and Vegetable Chow Mein

This stir-fried dish is common across China because it includes some of the most common ingredients cooks have in their kitchens. It can easily be made into a vegetarian recipe by leaving out the chicken or be expanded by adding different kinds of meat, such as beef and pork. Have an adult help you with this recipe.

Serves 4

Ingredients

3 tablespoons vegetable oil

1 teaspoon ginger, minced

1 pound chicken strips, cooked

1 carrot, cut into thin strips

1 green onion, cut into thin slices

1 green bell pepper, cut into thin strips

1 celery stalk, cut into thin slices

½ cup water chestnuts, drained and sliced

1 cup bean sprouts

8 ounces wheat noodles (spaghetti, linguini, or fettuccini), cooked

1 tablespoon soy sauce

Directions

With an adult's help, put a skillet or wok on high heat for 45 seconds. Add the oil. When it's hot, add the ginger, chicken, and all of the vegetables. Stir-fry for about 2 minutes. Add the noodles and soy sauce. Keep stirring until the noodles are separated and heated through. Remove and serve.

Midnight Snacks

If you're in the mood for a late-night snack in Taiwan, you're in luck. The streets are full of night markets. Vendors sell everything from oyster omelets and fruit ices to meat-filled buns and different flavors of bubble teas. Some favorite snacks include candied crab apples, squid on a stick, and *bao bing*, finely shaved ice pieces topped with peanuts, fruit, or condensed milk.

Touch the Heart

One of the most popular cusines throughout China is dim sum, which means "touch the heart." Dim sum are bite-size treats that can be made in hundreds of ways. Many of them are made with some kind of dough that is stuffed with a wide variety of ingredients. If they are fried crisp, they are called pot stickers. If they have paper-thin dough and are boiled in soup or broth, they are called wontons. Dim sum also includes small, individual portions of noodles, chicken feet, and steamed meatballs.

Dim sum are small, bite-size dishes prepared in a variety of ways.

Quitting Time!

Food is such an important part of the Chinese culture that it is referred to in many different sayings and in slang. For example, when a person decides to quit his or her job, it is referred to as "breaking the rice bowl."

Spring rolls are a favorite type of dim sum. Once prepared to celebrate the beginning of spring, they are now offered in all Chinese restaurants. The size of a finger, spring rolls have a paper-thin wrapper made from wheat or rice flour. The filling is made out of

A couple enjoys a variety of Chinese dishes in Hong Kong.

anything from shrimp or pork to bean sprouts and mushrooms. They are fried in vegetable oil and then dipped in either peanut or sweet and sour sauce.

These small treats make the perfect mid–morning or mid–afternoon snack. Special restaurants cater to dim sum fans, with waiters walking between the tables, pushing carts full of different treats to choose from.

With its light meals, variety of fresh vegetables, and mix of meat and other proteins, the Chinese diet is a relatively healthy one. The Chinese people, whose average life expectancy is seventy-three years, know how to make the most of what they have and eat simple but delicious meals.

Glossary

aristocratic   belonging to nobility

braise   to cook meat or vegetables by sautéing in fat and then simmering in liquid

Buddhism   a religion based on the teaching of Buddha

cuisine   a style or quality of cooking

dim sum   a variety of small dishes served individually

dynasties   a sequence of rulers from the same family or group

garnishes   things placed around or on food to add flavor and color

monsoons   wind systems that influence large climatic regions and reverse directions with the season

republic   a state in which the supreme power rests with the body of citizens entitled to vote

simmer   to cook in liquid kept at a state approaching boiling

steep   to let sit in hot water to extract flavor

tofu   bean curd made from soybeans

wok   a large, bowl-shaped pan used for cooking Chinese food

Find Out More

BOOKS

Goodman, Polly. *Food in China*. New York: PowerKids Press, 2008.

Hibbert, Clare. *China*. North Charleston, SC: Clara House Books, 2010.

Lee, Frances. *Fun with Chinese Cooking*. New York: PowerKids Press, 2009.

Locricchio, Matthew. *The Cooking of China*. New York: Marshall Cavendish Benchmark, 2012.

Mattern, Joanne. *Recipe and Craft Guide to China*. Hockessin, DE: Mitchell Lane, 2010.

McCulloch, Julie. *China*. Chicago: Heinemann Library, 2009.

DVD

Cooking with Kids: Exploring Chinese Food, Culture, and Language. Ni Hao Productions, 2006.

WEBSITES

Chinese Food: Teaching Culture through Cooking

http://chinesefood.about.com/od/resourceschinesecooking/a/
teachingcooking.htm

This site provides links to a variety of Chinese recipes that are
easy to make at home.

Chinese Food for Kids

www.china-family-adventure.com/chinese-food.html

Find out all about Chinese food, learn how to use chopsticks,
find recipes to try making at home, and much more.

Chinese New Year Games and Activities

www.apples4theteacher.com/holidays/chinese-new-year/

This resource links to fun Chinese stories, games, books, crafts,
and more that celebrate the culture and the New Year.

Index

Page numbers in **boldface** are illustrations and charts.

About the Author

Tamra Orr is the author of more than 250 books for readers of all ages. A graduate of Ball State University in Muncie, Indiana, Orr has a degree in secondary education and English and has written thousands of national and state assessment/test questions (hers are the ones you liked best!). Currently, she lives in the Pacific Northwest with her dog, cat, husband, and three teenagers. In her fourteen spare minutes each day, she loves to read, write letters, and travel around the state of Oregon, marveling at the breathtaking scenery.